A Solstice Tree for Jenny

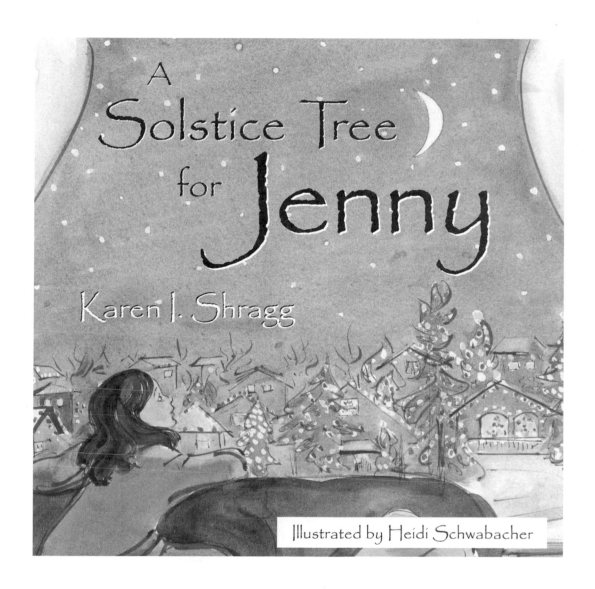

A Solstice Tree for Jenny

Karen I. Shragg

Illustrated by Heidi Schwabacher

Prometheus Books

59 John Glenn Drive
Amherst, New York 14228-2197

Published 2001 by Prometheus Books

Inquiries should be addressed to
Prometheus Books
59 John Glenn Drive
Amherst, New York 14228–2197
VOICE: 716–691–0133, ext. 207
FAX: 716–564–2711
WWW.PROMETHEUSBOOKS.COM

05 04 03 02 01   5 4 3 2 1

Library of Congress Cataloging-in-Publication Data

Shragg, Karen, 1954–
    A solstice tree for Jenny / Karen Shragg ; illustrated by Heidi Schwabacher.
        p. cm. — (Young readers series)
    Summary: Jenny feels left out when her parents, unlike the neighbors, do not observe any of the holidays in December, and so she and her family decide to create a celebration of the winter solstice that reflects their own beliefs.
    ISBN 1–57392–930–1 (alk. paper)
    [1. Holidays—Fiction. 2. Freedom of religion—Fiction. 3. Winster solstice—Fiction.
4. Conduct of life—Fiction.] I. Schwabacher, heidi, ill. II. Title. III. Young readers
(Amherst, N.Y.)

PZ7.S559145 So 2001
[Fic]—dc21   2001031618

Printed in the United States of America on acid-free paper

DEDICATION

FOR JOHN

THE WIND BENEATH MY HUMANIST WINGS

KAREN

FOR MY SUPPORT GROUP:

BILL, FAMILY, AND FRIENDS

HEIDI

It was Jenny's first December at home that she could ever remember. Her parents' work as archaeologists usually meant that Jenny spent the holiday season in some faraway part of the world. Making trips to dig out old city walls and temples during December was her parents' way of avoiding the holidays. Born into two different religions, they had long ago decided not to be a part of any religion. This year they had an important meeting in town, which meant that Jenny was home to see all the celebrations of Christmas, Hanukah, and Kwansaa.

On clear, crisp nights you could see the starry

winter sky from the living-room picture window in the house where Jenny lived with her mom and dad. As she knelt on the sofa and stared out of the window, Jenny could see at least five houses and even more in the distance. They didn't look especially interesting during the day, but at night, they were all dressed up in dazzling colors of blue, green, and red lights that glistened in reflections of freshly fallen snow. Big evergreen trees all aglow in tinsel and colorful ornaments decorated many frosted picture windows. One house had a big, blue and white Hanukah menorah with orange bulbs that dressed up its windowsill.

Jenny loved looking at the pretty decorations. They made the dark winter nights seem so cheery. She

really liked the blinking lights and the way some of her neighbors wrapped tree limbs and shrubs in white lights. In her house there were holiday cards on the closet door and a dinner table centerpiece of pine boughs and gold-colored candles, but her family had no pretty blinking lights, no ornament-covered Christmas tree or electric Hanukah menorah. Jenny was sure that hers had to be the ugliest house on the whole block. All the kids at school talked about decorating their trees or lighting their menorah candles, but Jenny felt left out of the holiday celebration talk.

"What do you do to for Christmas, Jenny?" one of her schoolmates asked.

"Most of the time we're not home in December. We're usually out of town," was all Jenny could say.

As she knelt on the sofa Jenny must have had a sad look in her eyes because her mother sat down beside her and asked, "Why the long face?"

Jenny responded with her own question, "How come we don't decorate our house with lights and stuff like our neighbors? Just look at how pretty their houses are," she said bluntly.

Mom hugged her and sighed. "We don't put up lights for Christmas, because it's not a holiday we celebrate; and we don't put up a Hanukah menorah, because we don't celebrate that holiday, either. We just try to take the wonderful things and special feelings we all seem to have this time of year and celebrate them," she tried to explain.

"But why can't we just put up lights because they're pretty and so we can look like all the other houses?" Jenny begged.

"Oh honey, I wish it were that simple . . . but the lights do mean something. Even though what we see on television and in department stores might have us believe that Christmas is a holiday that everyone in our country believes to be an important day, it really is a religious holiday celebrated by those who are Christians. That's where the name comes from. They are celebrating the birth of Jesus 'Christ' who they believe is the son of god," Mom answered. "Each holiday has a meaning behind it. Hanukah is celebrated by Jewish people, and has been a special holiday for over a thousand years. They believe that a long time ago their god saved them from being destroyed by their enemies. Kwansaa is a modern celebration. With symbols and candle lighting, African Americans concentrate on seven principles that are about building strong families and pride in their culture."

"But aren't the holidays just about being good to others and trying to be happy? And don't we believe in the same good things as all the other people on our block?" Jenny asked in a confused voice.

Her mother thought for minute. "Yes, of course we believe many of the same things our neighbors with the pretty lights believe. We have good neighbors and we share the way we each love our children and how we want this to be a safe and healthy place for our families to live. But our country is all about being free to believe or not believe in any religion as long as what we say and do doesn't hurt anybody else.

"Your father and I don't believe in a god that created the world and whose job it is to tell us how to live our lives. We think that we can be very good people and know what is right to do and not do without having to follow rules that some people believe were written down long ago by their god or by important people in their religion. Does this make sense to you, honey? I know that it's not easy to understand."

"I think I get it," Jenny said, wrinkling her forehead.

"Good, we can talk about this later, but you have school tomorrow and it's time for bed."

Jenny didn't sleep very well. She tossed and turned all night. She understood what her mother was saying, but it was just that, well, everyone was having so much fun with their holiday parties, plays, and caroling that it seemed to Jenny like there should be some way that her family could be a part of it all without really belonging to a religion. As Jenny drifted off to sleep she hoped that she could think of a way to have a celebration that was their very own. But when she woke up the next morning she was disappointed that no ideas had come to her while she was sleeping.

That day at school, Jenny went to see her reading teacher. Jenny was usually a very eager student, but she was distracted by her problem.

"You don't seem to be yourself today, Jenny. Is anything wrong?" her teacher wondered.

"I'm sorry, Ms. Montgomery. I was just trying to think up a new holiday celebration," Jenny mumbled, while doodling on a scratch pad.

"If I may ask, what's wrong with the ones we already have?" Ms. Montgomery asked.

"Oh, nothing, but my parents don't celebrate anything religious," Jenny said in an unusually sad voice.

"And in December, we have the ugliest house on the block because we don't have any pretty lights up or anything."

"I see," Ms. Montgomery replied. "Is there anything else that bothers you?" she asked.

"Well, yeah. I feel left out of all of the fun everyone is having," Jenny answered.

"I see. Well, I think it's not too surprising for a young girl like you to want to be a part of the fun your friends are having. It's good that you are trying to find an answer that will make both you and your parents happy. You're a very special girl, Jenny." Ms. Montgomery smiled as she looked over to her bookshelves. "Do you know about the winter solstice?"

"I think I've heard of it but I don't know what it means," Jenny answered.

"It's the time of year, on December 21st, when the northern half of our planet is turned the farthest away from the Sun. Many of the winter holidays, like Protestant and Catholic Christmas, Jewish Hanukah, and African American Kwansaa celebrations, often happen around the same time as this shortest day of the year, the winter solstice. Before these holidays were celebrated, there were many solstice celebrations in countries all over the northern half of the Earth. Candle lighting was the part of the celebration to help bring back the Sun in the days when they didn't know about the way the Earth tilts in its orbit around the Sun. They believed that lighting the candles would actually help bring back the Sun, since they did not fully understand that this was a part of the yearly journey of the Earth's orbit. They didn't know as much about the planets and how they move around the Sun as we do today. Remember when we talked about that when your class was learning about what's in outer space? I imagine that these festivals were a great way to cheer people up just when nature was at its gloomiest," Ms. Montgomery explained.

"So it's something that anyone can do?" Jenny asked.

"I would think so," Ms. Montgomery smiled. "Here's a book full of solstice stories. You are welcome to check it out and bring it back to me next week."

"Thank you, Ms. Montgomery. You're the best," Jenny said as she hugged her teacher and rushed out the door with the book under her arm.

Jenny couldn't keep her nose out of the winter solstice book. From what she could tell, the winter solstice comes once a year to this part of the world whether we celebrate it or not. It is something that people can celebrate if they want to and it is part of the way nature works. She learned that it is a way of marking time, just like spring is the time for planting and fall is the time for harvesting. She also learned that there are a few very old stone buildings that were built long ago as places to celebrate the winter solstice. *Winter Solstice Stories* told of people living long ago who thought of the Sun

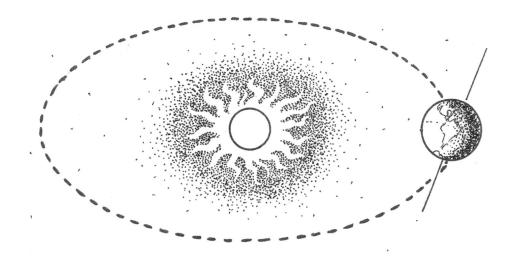

 as a god and made offerings to it to return and make the days longer so they could plant their crops. "They really needed a festival of lights," Jenny thought to herself.

❄   ❄   ❄

That night at the supper table, Jenny interrupted as her parents were talking about grown-up stuff.

"What do we believe in?" Jenny blurted.

"What do you mean, Jenny? And next time, please don't interrupt," her father scolded.

"I'm sorry, Daddy. But you told me we don't believe in a god and we don't go to church or anything, so what or who do we believe in?" she asked.

Jenny's parents looked at each other in that funny grown-up sort of way. Dad paused for a minute and then answered, "Of course we have beliefs, Jenny. Beliefs, even strong ones, don't have to come from a holy book, or be told to you in a church or a temple. You can believe in things just because they are important if you want to be a good person.

"You know how every year we help serve food to the homeless? That's because we believe in sharing what we have with others. And remember—"

"Hold on a second. Sorry, Daddy, that I didn't say 'excuse me,' but I want to write these down." Jenny ran to get a piece of paper. She couldn't write too well, but her printing was pretty good. With paper and

pencil in hand, she looked up at her father and said, "Okay, I'm ready, but don't go too fast."

"Remember those neighborhood meetings we had in our living room about saving the trees in Medford Park from road construction?" her fathered continued. "That's because we believe in protecting nature."

"We recycle and try to buy used things instead of new ones," Mom added, "because we believe in doing our part to help the environment.

"Each year we work on your school's fund-raiser because we believe in helping our schools. We send money to all kinds of helpful groups that try to make

the world a better place for everyone. We attend concerts and belong to museums because we believe that
music and art make life wonderful."

"And we do all these good things without being
religious or believing in a god?" Jenny asked looking
up from her notepad.

"Yes, dear," her parents said together.

"But I still don't get it. Don't our neighbors who
have all the pretty holiday lights believe in all of these
good things, too? I mean, the Nelsons are always
giving their old clothing and stuff to the poor and Mrs.
Kilborn is always collecting money from people on our
block for good causes. Why should it matter that they
believe their god wants them to do all of these good

things this time of year, just as long as we are all doing the same good things?" Jenny insisted.

"Some people believe that how they live is taught to them by their god, but we believe that having a good heart and living to help others can be learned and taught by one person showing another who shows another and so on," Mom tried harder to explain.

"But I still don't understand why I have to feel so different from my friends and our neighbors when it seems like we all just want the world to be a better place," Jenny sighed. "I don't like being different."

"That's a very good question, honey," her father said. "Many people pay more attention to who tells them to do good deeds rather than making sure they do what they should. We're often told by people who believe in a god that only religious people can do good things, and that just isn't so. We believe that what really counts is how we live our lives year-round. Lots of people feel they need a father who they often picture in a place far above them called heaven and he looks down on them to make sure they behave themselves. What they don't understand about our way of thinking is that they can just do good things because they are the right things to do. They can make people happy just by trying and not because they are afraid that their god will punish them if they don't do what he says. Also some people think that this god wants them to celebrate holidays in one way and others think that god wants them to celebrate in another way. When they don't agree, a lot of trouble can happen. Your mother and I think that all of this is important to know about, but we certainly didn't want you to feel bad because of it," he said.

"I think I understand, but how can things meant to be so good turn out to be so bad?" Jenny said.

"Religious celebrations do have good thoughts behind them, Jenny, but too often the arguments about who has the right idea of god and what he wants us to do, gets in the way of doing all those good things," her mother tried to explain.

"You mean like whether or not you celebrate

Christmas or Hanukah becomes more important than stuff like peace and love and having a warm place to sleep?" Jenny asked.

"That's pretty much it," Dad said.

"Well, if I ran the world," Jenny said, "it's just those good things we would care about."

Jenny's father smiled. "Well, honey, you just keep thinking that way and some day you might live in that wonderful world."

"Do you know about the winter solstice?" Jenny said, seeming to change the subject.

"That's when the Earth is tilted the furthest away from the Sun and our days are the shortest here in the north, isn't it?" her mother answered.

"Yeah, but it's a lot more than that," Jenny explained as she ran to get the book she borrowed from her teacher. Standing between her parents with the book open and turning to special pages to make her point, she said, "It's all about a time for festivals or parties when people from all over the northern part of the world would celebrate with special lights and foods. People held special dances and sang special songs because they thought that doing these things would bring back the Sun when the days were the darkest. I know we don't do stuff like that, but is there some way our family could make up our own solstice celebration, since everybody in our part of the Earth shares these days together and the solstice is a time to be glad that the days will get longer and spring is on the way?"

Jenny's parents agreed that creating their own winter solstice celebration would be just the thing to do. They admitted that they had some very happy memories of this time of year and those good times had nothing to do with religion, but had everything to do with feeling joy, spending time with their family, eating special foods, and looking forward to opening gifts. They didn't want Jenny to miss out on that. They all talked until it was time for Jenny to go to bed. Jenny's mom said she hoped they would not have to cut down a tree because she never liked seeing all of the dead trees on the curb after New Year's. Jenny's dad thought that they should decorate boxes for charity and put things in them that the poor and the homeless need. Jenny thought that they could light candles on the solstice and share a favorite story about how important this time of year is for them. They all agreed that presents would be good as long as they weren't too expensive. Mom thought that the best gifts they could give each other would be doing things together like going to plays and concerts and on vacations, or giving books. Dad said that they should make a list of their favorite foods and make them for a special dinner. As the evening wore on, Jenny's parents had to admit that they missed this part of the holidays. They were glad to have the excitement back in their lives of planning a celebration. No one could quite figure out

what they would decorate. They did know that they wanted it to be a living thing, so they decided to take a trip to the local garden center on the weekend. Jenny could hardly wait for Saturday to come. The week just seemed to drag on and on.

The weekend finally arrived and they jumped into the car and headed for the garden center. During the drive Jenny's dad looked up in the rearview mirror and caught Jenny's eye.

"You know, Jenny, we should've done this a long time ago. It's much more fun to make our own special time together than to try to avoid everyone else's. Thank you for helping us understand that it's important to create our own celebration around all the things that are important to us." Jenny just smiled.

They walked up and down the aisles of the garden center, not exactly knowing what they were looking for. Just when Jenny was about to give up, her eyes fell upon a small potted tree.

"THERE it is," she shouted. Sitting in a corner wrapped in a red velvety cloth was the prettiest little potted pine tree that Jenny had ever seen.

"Oh, it's perfect, isn't it? It's just the right size to put in our living room and decorate with these little signs." Jenny pulled out a few of the little pieces of paper she had stuffed in her pockets. On one she had written the words, "We believe in education," and on another, "We believe in helping people." Not every

word was spelled correctly, but that didn't seem to stop Jenny's mom from shedding a few happy tears.

"Oh, Jenny, you are something else," her father beamed.

"Can we please get it? It's even on sale!" Jenny begged.

Jenny's mom looked at the label of the little Norfolk Island Pine. "Well, I like that it's a living tree, but that does mean it needs to be cared for. Will you help remember to water it?" she asked Jenny.

"I promise!" Jenny said eagerly.

When they got home, they placed the three-foot-tall tree on a table covered with a shimmering gold tablecloth. They put the table in front of the picture window in the living room where it could be easily seen by anyone passing by.

They all spent the afternoon decorating their new solstice tree with little white lights to remember the candles and torches of solstice celebrations years ago. The tree was trimmed with special messages of hope, good will, and kindness. That night, long after everyone had gone to bed, Jenny snuck out of her bedroom to take a peek at their tree. It was so beautiful, all lit up with her hand-printed colored papers dangling from green yarn on its branches. Underneath the tree Jenny had placed a box she decorated herself, marked "Food Shelf" and a beautiful glass jar bank with the words "Save the Trees" on it. She reached up and

added one more saying to the top of the tree: "You can celebrate the winter solstice no matter who you are." It seemed to stand so tall for such a little tree. Jenny felt so proud. She could hardly wait to have her friends over and show them her beautifully decorated solstice tree and share its story.

"We don't have the ugliest house on the block anymore," she thought to herself. In fact, it was the best tree anyone could have because the messages on its branches could be shared with everyone, whether they believed in a god or not. "And," Jenny said to herself, "if I take really good care of our little solstice tree, it will be around till the next winter solstice, bigger and better than ever."